Charlene the Star and

Bentley Bulldog

By Deanie Humphrys-Dunne

Illustrated by Holly Humphrys-Bajaj

Printed in the United States

Dedication for Charlene the Star and Bentley Bulldog

This book is dedicated to Sarah, Yael, Janice, Alicia and Geri, beautiful, gifted ladies who are remarkable in every way. Thank you all for your constant support.

Ernie,

Bentley is
so naughty
but his new
friends help
him behave.
We hope you
like his story.

Deanie

The Bully

Introduction:

"Hi, my name is Charlene the Star. I'm a horse who loves jumping. I'm kicking up my heels while Mary's riding me. I'm excited. I'm preparing for a big jumping competition in a few weeks. I live at Jumping for Joy Farms. I adore jumping but I was getting flabby from not practicing enough during my vacation. It could be I'm a little chubby from too many peppermints Mary gives me when I do something well. Last year I won the Green Jumper Championship at the Sterling Horse Show. This year I want to win the award for being the best jumper in the whole state of Kentucky."

Charlene thought, *Mary's galloping me toward the in and out jump. I need to pay attention because there are one or two strides between the two jumps and if we don't measure them right, we'd be in trouble. Mary* uses her *long*

*legs to help me adjust my stride before the jumps. We're in
and we took one nice long stride and we're out. We were
perfect. Mary's patting my pretty red coat, so I know she's
happy with my work.*

Charlene thought, *I see a funny-looking dog sitting next
to the ring. He barked at me so I stopped to look at him.
He's plump with wrinkles and he has a pouty face.*

"Charlene, you stopped so quickly you almost made me
fall off," Mary said. "I bumped my chin against your neck.
You even made my riding hat bounce around on my head.
What's going on? Maybe you wanted to say hello to the
dog who's watching us jump. I've never seen him before.
He's wearing a colorful collar and tag that says his name is
Bentley. I wonder if he wants to stay here. We'll have to
advertise to find his owners. He doesn't have a big head or
big brindle spots like Elliott does. But he's still a rather
handsome dog."

Charlene thought, *my friends and I can talk to other animals, but we don't talk to people. Mary's walking me, or cooling me off, before we go back to the barn. That's important because if she put me in the barn when I was sweaty, I could get sick.*

"Charlene, here's what I'm going to do: fix your dinner, feed Elliott and Bentley. I'll put the dishes outside the door for Elliott and our visitor. Nice job today, Charlene, even though you gave me extra excitement when you stared at the new dog," said Mary.

"Elliott, can you chat with Bentley? He doesn't seem too friendly. Perhaps he'd rather get acquainted with you first," said Charlene.

"Of course Charlene, but first I'm going across the street to escort Hattie the Chicken so she can meet Bentley. I give her rides on my back to keep her safe. It's hard to see her when she's crossing the street, even though she always wears her bonnet. I'm really hungry, but it's important to think of Hattie. She'll be hopping around with excitement when she meets Bentley," said Elliott. He thought, *I have to look both ways carefully before I cross the street. I love protecting Hattie. She's such a special little chicken and she's talented as well.*

"Hi, Charlene," said Hattie as she carefully hopped off Elliott's back. "I had to adjust my pretty red bonnet in case it got jostled during my ride on Elliott."

***

"Who's the new dog?" asked Hattie jumping around, flapping her wings with excitement.

Bentley jumped in front of her, sticking his head in front of Hattie's face.

"I'm Bentley. It's silly to see a chicken wearing a bonnet," Bentley said, laughing loudly. "Chickens can't do anything. Have you ever heard of anyone talking about a chicken's outstanding skills? No! Nobody even mentions them unless they're on the dinner menu."

"Excuse me, but chickens, with or without bonnets, deserve respect," Hattie answered. "You have no reason to laugh at me. Yes, I do have abilities! For example, I'm a good organizer with neat beakmanship. (It's like handwriting.) My beakmanship helped us win the Coaches of the Year Award. My friends and I all worked as a team. We showed people we could accomplish amazing things together. Hattie was so upset the feathers on her back stood straight up. She stared straight into Bentley's eyes. "By the way, are you a professional bully? You're good at bullying, but I wouldn't be proud of that, if I were you. You should also know that I love wearing bonnets because they help me feel special." Hattie ruffled her red feathers in frustration. "Bentley, you need to learn some manners." Hattie thought, *He's the rudest animal I've ever met.*

"I'm sorry, Hattie; but my mom was too busy to teach me good manners. I have seven siblings. I'm terribly embarrassed," said Bentley, covering his face with his paws.

"Hattie, I'm proud of you for standing up to Bentley when he teased you. You were remarkably brave. I was ready to come to your rescue, but you did a great job on your own," said Elliott. *I'm lucky Bentley didn't say something about my oversized head. Maybe that's because his is quite large too.*

"Thank you, Elliott. Earlier today I was wondering what to do if standing up to a bully like Bentley doesn't work. Do you have any ideas?" asked Hattie.

"Hattie, remember what a special chicken you are. Then unkind words won't hurt you," answered Elliott.

"Elliott, you shared excellent advice. Now mean words won't hurt my feelings," said Hattie.

Elliott thought, *I can't wait for dinner. I worked up an appetite escorting Hattie. Mary always mixes it just right whether I get vegetables with rice dog food or something else. Bentley is standing in front of my dinner. He doesn't look like he intends to move soon. Maybe he's applying for squatter's rights. That's permission to stay, if you're the first one to claim the property, I'll try the polite approach.*

"Bentley I'm hungry. You're interrupting my dinner hour. Would you mind moving aside so I can have my meal? You're welcome to the other food," said Elliott, hoping to end the standoff.

"I eat every dinner in sight. How do you think I got my stout shape?" replied Bentley, patting his round tummy. "I've always practiced my bullying skills. No one ever challenged me."

"Bentley, we have rules here. We only eat what belongs to us. I could say more about your horrid manners, but I'll keep quiet and set a good example." *It looks like he's going to be reasonable. Thankfully, there's no need for a new plan.*

Bentley thought, *I'm completely befuddled for the first time in my life. No one ever stood up to me before. I've always been a bully, but I haven't been a happy dog. Maybe it's time to change my ways.*

"My apologies, Elliott. I'm grateful for the other dinner and you're welcome to yours," said Bentley, covering his face. *I thought the words would get stuck in my throat, but they sounded pretty good. Nothing bad happened either.*

Jumping Around

"Good morning, Charlene," said Mary, brushing strands of blond hair away from her forehead. "Tomorrow's the big day when we'll be competing in the Sterling Club Horse Show. This time we'll be entering the Open Jumper Classes, so the competition will be tough. We've worked hard to make sure we're ready. Of course, Elliott will come to keep you calm and Bentley will join us. It's a shame no one answered our ad looking for his owners. But he seems to be settling in well here."

I see Eva, my groom, walking into the barn. She wants to be sure I look spectacular for the big day tomorrow. Eva will braid my mane (the hair on my neck) too. She'll bathe me so my soft red coat covering my body, is almost glowing. I want to act like a star tomorrow. That doesn't mean I'm not humble. I'm grateful for my natural gifts. What a shame they can't give me a prize for having the

prettiest red hair but, I have to earn my awards. It makes
them more special.

"Bentley, I hope you enjoy your first horse show. Elliott will be sure to show you proper manners. As you can see, he's so relaxed he's practically falling asleep," said Charlene.

"Thank you so much for bringing me to the show today, Elliott. I have one big concern," Bentley stated. "When I looked out the window, I didn't see any doggie snack bars. Did they hide them somewhere? Why would dogs come without snack bars? They mustn't have a dog on the committee making the rules. I think the people in charge should think of everyone, especially bulldogs."

"I didn't see any either, Bentley. But I think you can survive without snacking for one day. We'll be too busy to think about eating. Our job is to cheer for Charlene when she's jumping. When she's resting we'll make sure she stays calm," said Elliott.

"Let's settle in on the bleachers. It's almost time for Charlene's class to start. Bentley, you're taking up the whole row," Elliott said, gently pushing him over. "Stop being selfish and leave me some space so I'll be comfortable, too." Elliott stared into Bentley's eyes.

"I'm sorry, Elliott. I must've been thinking like a bully. I'm an English bulldog so I'm famous for being stubborn. The American bulldogs look kind of wimpy to me. Truthfully, I like being sturdy. Did you know I was named for the expensive English car called the Bentley? My former owners had one. When I rode in it, I felt important when I stuck my head out the window and felt the wind against my face. The car was quite reliable and handsome, like me. Sorry if I seem a bit overconfident here. After all, I was pampered. I'm yawning thinking of how boring my life was. All I did was go to the pet salon for grooming. I left in search of adventure. I think I found it."

***

"Charlene, you look gorgeous this morning with your adorable braids neatly done. I must give Eva a compliment when I see her," Mary said. She quickly tightened the blue ribbon at the end of her own braid.

"I'm glad we went into the warm-up ring to get you settled down before our class. You know that's where we go to warm your muscles up so you can do your best in your class. Ah, you're tossing your head to show me you're ready for jumping," said Mary.

"Ladies and gentlemen, our next competitor is number fifty-one, Charlene the Star, ridden by Mary Harris. You may remember they were Green Jumper Champions last year," said the announcer.

Wow, the jumps are higher than last year. I'll try not to rush so we do our best. There are post and rail jumps, and a water jump, or Liverpool, just to mention a few. The Liverpool is the one with blue plastic with water in it. The name "Liverpool," makes me think it's a pool full of liver, yuck. Elliott and Bentley are barking for us. It's great that Elliott is training Bentley well. I see Bentley and Elliott giving each other high fives. They're celebrating for us.

The announcer said, "Ladies and gentlemen, Charlene the Star had a clean round with no faults. Congratulations to Charlene and Mary."

"Great job, Charlene, you jumped like a star today," said Mary, patting Charlene's glossy red coat. "Now we'll see if anyone else has a clear round. If they do, we'll have to jump again. It's called a jump-off. The horse and rider with fewer faults in the fastest time will be the winner."

"Charlene, you're prancing around while we're waiting for the judge's decision," Mary said. "I'll bet you're impatient."

Charlene thought, *Mary did a good job guessing I was nervous about waiting. My beautiful coat is sweaty because I'm feeling anxious.*

"The judges have made their decision. First place goes to number fifty-one, Charlene the Star, ridden by Mary Harris," said the announcer.

"Charlene, I'm so proud of you," Mary said, jumping up and down. "You'll get extra peppermints tonight." *Thinking of my peppermints makes me even happier. I don't mind working hard to earn them.*

"All horses and riders entered in the Open Jumper Stakes Class, please report to ring two immediately," said the announcer.

Goody, the Open jumper Stakes is the one where you win money. I love to help Mary earn money.

"Ladies and gentlemen, our next competitor is Charlene the Star, ridden by Mary Harris," said the announcer.

Charlene thought, *It's a different course now. There's a gate jump and a jump with colorful barrels in front of it. There's also an oxer or spread jump. It looks like two jumps pushed together. Who's the stunning black horse standing by the rail? Yikes, I was so distracted I knocked down the gate jump! Ouch, it hurt my legs. I guess it doesn't pay to be gawking at the most handsome horse in the world when I should be working. I felt my heart thumping, just looking at him. I wonder if this is love. I'm tossing my head and doing little stiff-legged bucks called crow hops because I'm mad at myself for not paying attention.*

"Charlene, what on earth happened? What were you looking at?" asked Mary, stunned by Charlene's mistake. "I see you've lowered your head. I'll bet you're embarrassed about what just occurred. We all make mistakes. We'll try to improve our performance next time. She patted Charlene's neck.

"Ladies and gentlemen, we have a tie between Charlene the Star, ridden by Mary Harris and Presiding Judge, ridden by Kayla Moran. We'll have a jump-off to determine the winner," said the announcer. "Number fifty-one, Charlene the Star, will jump first."

Charlene thought, *I'll call the handsome black horse Judge for short. I wonder which one of us will win. So far, we're perfect. We only have the oxer left to jump. Oops, I just touched one rail. It's bouncing around the brackets holding the poles. Oh, darn. It fell down. I tried my* best, but nobody wins all *the time. I'm still proud of my efforts. Mary's patting me on the neck, so I did a good job.*

"We'll have to wait to see what Presiding Judge does. He's jumping now. Wow, he had a clean round," said Mary.

"Ladies and gentlemen, we have our winner. First place goes to number 103, Presiding Judge, ridden by Kayla Moran with no faults. Second place is number fifty-one, Charlene the Star, ridden by Mary Harris, with a total of four faults," said the announcer.

If I didn't concentrate on my work, I wouldn't be proud of myself. Otherwise, my peppermints might be restricted. I love the feeling that I tried my best, even if I didn't win. That's why I'm holding my head high. Now I'll have lunch and take a short nap.

Charlene thought, *Lunch and my nap were heavenly. I had time to rest my legs. Bentley is sitting outside making sure no one disturbs me so I'll do amazingly well in my next class.*

There's a commotion outside. Bentley's barking. Is he trying to protect me from an intruder? No, I have a visitor. It's Judge! Butterflies are fluttering in my tummy. Do I look my best? Do I have dust on me? I'll shake a little, just in case I have any dust on me, but I'll be careful not to disturb my cute braids How I should act when I have a gentleman caller?

"Hey," said Judge, "I thought I'd stop by to say hello. I snuck away because Kayla forgot to tie me in the trailer. I guess she'll be lookin' for me soon. Anyway, I wanted to say how talented you are. I was surprised when you knocked down the gate in the Stakes Class. What happened?"

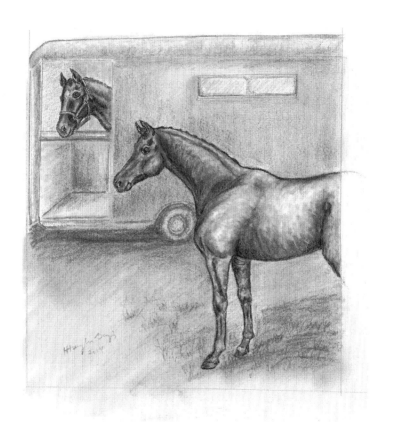

The First Date

"I crashed through the jump because I was staring at

you. You're the handsomest horse I've ever seen. I wasn't

paying attention to the jump," said Charlene, lowering her head, and keeping her voice at a whisper.

"I've never seen a redhead as pretty as you, either. I'd like to learn more about you. Maybe we'll become a couple. Wouldn't that be exciting?" asked Judge, not acting the least bit shy. "I should go back to the trailer before Kayla puts out an alert."

"I'd like getting to know you better, too. Meanwhile, I look forward to competing against you again. Thanks for stopping by," Charlene said.

Wow, it was exciting to have Judge come to visit. I tried to be composed on our secret date. I'd like to be perfectly calm like he is, instead of always fretting about things.

"Charlene, we must get ready for our last class, the Open Jumper Classic. It will be difficult, but we'll both focus on doing our best," said Mary, backing Charlene out of the trailer.

Charlene thought, *I watched Judge take the course. He did okay, but he had a refusal. That means he stopped at a jump. The refusal cost him three faults. I wonder if he was distracted thinking of our first date together.*

The announcer said I'm next. Here we go. We finished the oxer and the in and out; so far so good. Here's the water jump with the little picket fence in front of it. I'm building up some speed to avoid stepping in the water. I slipped a little, but still didn't step in the water, thank goodness. There's one jump left. It's a post and rail with barrels in front of it. There are pretty flower boxes on the sides, too. They look good enough to eat, but I can't think of that when I'm working. I remember what happened last time. Mary must be focusing on her work. She's not talking. I just touched the rail with my front foot, but it didn't fall. I hear Elliott and Bentley barking. I'll bet they're thrilled with our performance.

"Ladies and gentlemen, Charlene the Star and Mary Harris had no faults. That's amazing, considering how challenging this course is," said the announcer. "Mary's pleased. She's kissing Charlene's neck."

"Good job, Charlene," Mary whispered, hugging Charlene's neck. "You're going to have a peppermint party tonight."

Imagine a party where peppermints get top billing. I should get plenty of them after winning today.

"Ladies and Gentlemen, we're pleased to announce that our Open Jumper Champion today is Charlene the Star, ridden by Mary Harris, with a total of thirteen points. Our Reserve Champion with eleven points is Presiding Judge, ridden by Kayla Moran. The reserve champion is the horse and rider with the second highest number of points. We certainly had a close competition today," said the announcer.

"Look at this beautiful trophy, Charlene, "said Mary. "You should be proud, but there is always room for improvement. Staying focused on your work all the time would help. If you want to be the best in the state and win the High Score Award you'll have to concentrate on doing your best."

Mary's right about that, but she'd understand if she knew I was staring at Judge. I'm going to think about the good things that happened today, like my first date and second championship. Imagine how excited I'd feel if I won the High Score Award.

Bentley the Hero

"Bentley, why don't you put on your orange crossing guard jacket and we'll go across the street to meet Wooliam? I'm taller so I don't need the orange jacket to be noticed as much as you do. Wooliam is a sweet, friendly sheep. He created Wooliam's Lemonade Shack with some of our friends," said Elliott.

"I can barely fit into my orange coat. Maybe we should do some push-ups, or jogging, so I can get in shape. Would exercise work instantly? I'd love to see Hattie again. I slipped a note for her into the little pocket of my coat," Bentley said.

"Eating only <u>one</u> dinner with no snacks would do wonders for your weight," said Elliott.

"It would be a huge adjustment trying to survive on one dinner, but it might work. Do you think I'd feel faint?"

"Somehow, I don't think that's a big concern," said Elliott, sporting his biggest smile. "Look carefully before you cross the street, Bentley."

"I'll be careful. I hope there isn't much traffic. My stubby legs don't like to hurry. Truthfully, running would be a new experience," said Bentley, feeling a bit embarrassed.

"Just put one short leg in front of the other and you'll be on the other side in no time," said Elliott. "Wait! I see a car coming. I'll hold my paw out and direct traffic while you cross the street. That's it, just keep walking, Bentley. Good job! Now I'll finish crossing the street myself."

***

Bentley thought, *Now we're across the street and in the barn. I'll give Hattie my note. I wanted her to feel better after I was mean to her the first time we met.*

"Hello, Bentley, I'm surprised to see you," said Hattie, unsure of what to expect.

"Hi Hattie, I have a note for you. But it's the first one I've ever written so don't expect much," said Bentley, feeling more shy than he expected.

"What a lovely gesture, thank you. May I read it now?" Hattie asked, flapping her wings at the thought of getting a letter.

"If ya want," answered Bentley.

"I can't wait," said Hattie, hopping up and down, with glee.

Hattie opened Bentley's letter with her beak. It said, *Bentley's sorry he acted like a jerk. A chicken might make a good friend. He'd try to make it up to me.*

"Thank you, Bentley," said Hattie. "I appreciate your thoughtful note. It would be an honor to call you my friend." Hattie patted Bentley on his back with her wing.

"Aw, thanks, Hattie," said Bentley. "I could get used to those little pats with your wing. If I didn't have a pouty face, I'd smile. But I'm smiling on the inside."

"I hear hoof beats. What's happening? Someone's in a hurry to get here," said Elliott. "Oh, hello Wooliam, I didn't recognize you at first because you galloped by so fast.

"It's nice to see you. This is Bentley Bulldog."

"Good to meet you, Bentley," said Wooliam, still catching his breath.

"I've never seen a sheep with black legs and a black face. I'm not teasing you. I think it's unusual," said Bentley.

"I'm a Suffolk sheep. My whole family has the same markings," said Wooliam. "Has anyone seen the headline in the Gazette this morning?"

"No" replied everyone together.

"The headline said, "Depression Spreading Among Chickens!" The article went on to say chickens are feeling sad because they think they have no talent. Besides, they feel like they never have fun," said Wooliam.

"Horrors, I'm feeling dizzy," said Hattie, wobbling as she walked. Bentley rushed to her rescue.

"Thank you for escorting me to the chair so carefully, Bentley," she whispered. "We must plan an event to help the chickens." Hattie fanned herself, as she tried to recover from the shocking news.

"Wooliam, can you set up your Wooliam and Friends Lemonade Shack and sell some of your marvelous drinks?" asked Hattie.

"Of course, Hattie. There's new, yummy pink lemonade we can sell along with our original flavor. I'm sure we'll raise lots of money to help your friends."

"I can make some of my beautiful bonnets and matching purses. Naturally, they're originals. I'll sign them so people will know I made them," said Hattie, feeling pleased with her idea.

"Bentley, what would you like to make for the fair?" asked Elliott. "We haven't discussed your abilities yet."

"I have excellent math skills. I can add numbers in my head," said Bentley. But what could I do with that?"

"Can we have a demonstration, please?" asked Elliott. "Bentley, can you add: 144, plus 3002, plus 566?

"Sure, the answer is 3,712."

"Amazing, would you like to be our accountant? You could also collect the money at the fair," said Elliott.

"Definitely, but can I make something to sell at the fair as well?"

I ought to do something nice and learn to work with other animals. We never practiced working together when I acted like a bully. "Actually, I've had experience as a stone mason. I can make things out of stone. Can I make a statue for the fair? *I have a great idea. I'll keep it a secret until the last minute.*

"That's fantastic Bentley," said Elliott. "Hattie, would you write an ad for the fair and put it in *The Gazette?*

"I would love to design something special and draw a picture of our group so animals will know we're all involved in helping to cheer up the chickens," said Hattie.

"We must also mention that our fair will be sponsored by the Save the Chickens Foundation."

"Don't forget to add my picture. I'd love animals to know I'm not a bully anymore."

"Elliott, please ask Charlene if she would like to be involved with our fair."

"Of course, Hattie, I'm sure Charlene would be delighted to help you," answered Elliott.

"We can have a talent show for the chickens. They'll love it. I'll put some posters up around town. Elliott, can you help? We can work together like we've done before. We were a great team," said Hattie, hopping in circles with excitement.

"Certainly, Hattie, I'd be honored to help. I can't wait to see your ad in the Gazette," said Elliott. "Bentley, we should cross the street before it gets dark. We must start planning for our fair."

***

Hattie and Elliott went to the barn to share the news with Charlene.

"Charlene, Hattie was beside herself when she heard about the headline in *The Gazette*. Chickens are feeling sad because they're not having fun and they don't think they have any skills. We decided we'd plan a fair to cheer them up," said Elliott. "Do you think you could donate some copies of your book, *Charlene the Star?* Everyone would love their important message and adorable pictures."

"Of course, I'd love to help raise money for the well-being of chickens," said Charlene. "I'd even sign my books. I'd hold the pen in my teeth. Signed books are even more special, I think. Let me know if you need anything else."

"Wonderful, we'll tell Hattie so she can include information about your books in her ad," said Bentley.

Trouble for Charlene

"Good morning, everyone. I've finished our ad for the fair," said Hattie, hopping around, flapping her wings. "Check this out:

Come to our Fair! Cheer up the Chickens:

"Featuring items made by Hattie the Chicken, delicious lemonade from Wooliam and Friends Lemonade Shack, signed books by Charlene the Star, a surprise item designed by Bentley Bulldog, a raffle, and a talent show! Call 1-800-Hattie 4U."

"It's perfect, Hattie," said Charlene. "I'm entered in another show tomorrow called the Kentucky Bluegrass Show. I hope we have nice weather for it. Mary and I have been jumping new things like brick walls and rails with flowers in front of them. I guess Mary doesn't want me to be scared of odd-looking jumps."

Charlene thought, *Elliott, Bentley and I are riding to the show. Unfortunately, the weather is horrible. It's pouring sheets of rain but at least I have my rain shoes on so I'm less likely to slip in the mud. Jumping in the mud isn't much fun, but I've done it before, so I should be fine.*

"Charlene, we're only going to warm up and take a couple of jumps. I don't want you getting too tired. It takes more energy for you to jump in the mud," Mary said. "I don't want you catching cold, either. We'll walk over to the ring now because our class is about to start.

"All horses and riders entered in the Open Jumper Class, please report to the gate of ring one," said the announcer.

"Our first competitor is number twenty- seven, Presiding Judge, ridden by Kayla Moran," said the announcer.

Judge seems happy today. He's kicking up his heels, as if he can't wait to start jumping. He doesn't have any faults yet. Only three jumps left. Oops, he knocked down the last jump. How disappointing for him. I may not do better than that in this weather.

"Ladies and Gentlemen, please welcome number seventy-three, Charlene the Star, ridden by Mary Harris," said the announcer.

Here we go. I'm a little worried about jumping in the mud, but I'll do my best. I'll be proud of myself no matter what happens. We jumped the gate, the stonewall and the water jump. Here's the oxer, no faults yet. My front foot feels strange. I wonder what happened. We only have the in and out. We made it with no faults! I'm warm and I'm sneezing, plus my foot hurts. I'd like to go home and take a nap. I can hear Elliott and Bentley barking in the stands. I'm glad they're sitting under a big umbrella.

"Charlene, I'm proud of you for doing well. You feel strange, though. I think you're limping. Let me check your foot. Ah, you've lost a front shoe. You were brave to finish jumping without your shoe. I think that's why you're lame. You might've bruised your foot. I'll take you to the blacksmith. He's the one who fixes your feet and fits you with new shoes. There is always a blacksmith at shows, just in case any of the horses lose their shoes," Mary said.

"Hello, Mr. Shoemaker my horse, Charlene the Star, lost her left front shoe and she's lame in that foot. Would you put another shoe on, please?" asked Mary.

"Sure, I see her foot is broken up. She probably bruised it when she was jumping in the mud. I'll put a pad under the shoe to give her some cushion when she walks. She'll feel more comfortable in a few days."

"Thank you, Mr. Shoemaker. She's sneezing and shivering. As soon as you're finished, I'm going to take her home. She seems to be catching a cold. I'll cancel the rest of Charlene's classes today," said Mary.

While Mr. Shoemaker was fixing Charlene's shoe, Mary walked over to the show secretary's tent to speak with Mrs. Whitney. "Hello, Mrs. Whitney, my name is Mary Harris. My horse, Charlene the Star, isn't feeling well so I'm going to cancel the rest of her classes. The Open Jumper Class we competed in is still going on. If we should win a ribbon, would you please mail it to my house? You have my address on the registration."

"Of course, Miss Harris I'll be happy to send the ribbon if you win one. I'm sorry that your horse is not well. I'll also mail you a refund for the classes in which you couldn't compete," said Mrs. Whitney.

"Thank you for being so helpful, Mrs. Whitney," said Mary, brushing some wet strands of hair away from her face.

***

Charlene thought, *Now we're in the trailer, on the way home from the show. I feel yucky. I think Mary will call Dr. Howard in the morning if I'm not feeling better. I'm sneezing and coughing, but at least my foot feels better. It's a shame that we had to leave early. I won't be able to earn any more points toward the High Score Award from that show. Maybe Judge will earn many more than I have. I wonder if I can catch up.*

Mary dried Charlene's coat off with a thick towel before she put a warm blanket on her. "I hope you sleep well tonight, Charlene. I'll put some oats in your feed bin with a couple of peppermint candies. I hope you eat your dinner, otherwise I'll be worried," Mary said.

"Charlene, I'll sleep in your stall tonight. You might rest better if I'm there," said Elliott.

"Thanks, Elliott. You're such a special friend."

Charlene and Elliott rested during the night. When the sun peeked through the window of her stall the next morning Mary came in to check on her favorite patient.

"Poor Charlene, you didn't finish breakfast this morning. You even left the peppermint candies on top of the oats. That never happens. I'll call our veterinarian right away," said Mary, looking very concerned. "You remember when he came to see you when you were ill before, don't you, Charlene?"

Soon Dr. Howard's red pickup truck bounced along the gravel driveway. He came in and started his examination of Charlene.

"Dr. Howard, now that you've checked out Charlene, what's your opinion?" asked Mary, patting Charlene's neck.

"She has a bad cold and a slight fever. Charlene will need to rest for at least a week; just to be sure she's recovered. She could develop bronchitis, if she doesn't get complete rest. I've given her some antibiotics, so she should feel much better in a few days. It'll give her foot some time to heal. Be sure to call me right away if she seems listless or doesn't have her usual appetite," said Dr. Howard.

"Thank you so much. I'll be sure to call immediately if Charlene doesn't improve. Charlene, I hope you feel better soon and eat your breakfast," said Mary.

"Elliott, let's take a nap together. Maybe when we wake up I'll feel much better," said Charlene, yawning. Elliott patted Charlene on her neck when they snuggled up together.

"Thank you for the little pats, Elliott. They're helping me feel better," said Charlene.

"It was nothin', Charlene," Elliott answered.

The next day when Mary visited Charlene she was pleased to see that Charlene had finished every oat in her feed bin.

"Are you feeling better, this morning, Charlene? I see you ate your breakfast. Good girl," said Mary, feeling relieved. "But you're still coughing. Since it's a warm sunny day the sunshine might ease your cold. We'll walk out to the pasture where you can nibble on some grass. Elliott is with us to make sure you're staying relaxed and enjoying the weather."

"The sun feels good Elliott. Now that I'm taking a rest from the shows, we can spend more time planning our fair. Look, Bentley's escorting Hattie across the street. He remembered to wear his orange jacket," said Charlene. "I'll bet they want to discuss the fair."

Bentley Escorting Hattie

"Hi everyone, I couldn't wait to visit today," said Hattie, hopping about with glee. "Bentley was kind enough to escort me across the street on his back. Exciting things are happening regarding our plans for the fair. We're going to have a program listing the chickens who will be in the talent show. We'll also include names of those who are doing special things for the event. Patsy Pig will bake blueberry pies and muffins for a bake sale. She's thrilled about it."

"Cherish Chicken was the first contestant to enter the talent show. She's going to sing. She's shy, especially now that she's wearing glasses. Her friend, Betty Lee Chicken, is going to tap dance in the show. Another contestant is Carson Chicken, who's going to read a poem that he wrote. It'll be such fun and my friends will feel more important, as well," said Hattie, flapping her wings. "Wooliam, I'm sorry, I hardly noticed you. I'm excited about our event," she added.

"I understand, it sounds marvelous, Hattie. We're all planning to help make the fair a big success for your friends. I've spoken with the Ladies Group of Sheep and they've agreed to make a beautiful quilt from my wool. They did a fantastic job on the blanket they made from my wool last year," said Wooliam. "I'm getting my wool shaved this afternoon and the ladies will stop by to pick it up. Did you notice my wool is especially soft? I always use Wool Brite on it so it's perfect for special occasions like the fair."

"You do look particularly handsome this morning, Wooliam," said Hattie.

"Here's Charlene, and Elliott. I heard they were sleeping in this morning because Charlene was feeling ill," said Hattie. "We should remind her to rest so she'll be feeling better on the day of the fair."

"Hi everyone, are we having a meeting about the fair?" asked Charlene.

"Yes, Hattie said plans are coming along well. We should put some fliers up today. I believe Hattie, Elliott and Bentley have already volunteered to help with that," said Wooliam. "By the way, how are you feeling, Charlene?"

"Thanks for asking, Wooliam. I'm feeling better today, but Dr. Howard said I need to rest until my cold and my foot feel better," answered Charlene, trying not to yawn.

"You can nap soon, Charlene. Hattie, Elliott and Bentley will put up some posters that Hattie designed. They're so cute with our picture on them. They'll put the posters up after we finish our meeting."

"Well, I think we've made all the plans so we can end the meeting now," said Hattie, hopping around. "I can't wait for the fair. I'm making a beautiful bonnet for the big day. By the way, Elliott, you look handsome wearing your tool belt."

"Why, thank you, Hattie. I have some painter's tape in it so we can put up the posters without harming anything," replied Elliott. "I didn't want to bring nails because people would complain about damage from the holes."

"Excellent idea, Elliott," said Hattie, flapping her wings.

"Hattie, can you reach the store window? It would be a great place for a flier," said Bentley.

"No, I can't Bentley. Let's see if I can reach it if you're standing on the bench in front of the window with me your back." Hattie climbed onto Bentley's back while the bulldog stretched as high as he could. "It's very close, but I can't quite reach high enough. I've got an idea. If I hop on to your head, Bentley, I think I'll be little higher. Hattie hopped on Bentley's head. "Now I'm just right. I'll sign the flier so everyone will know I'm the designer. I'm pleased it says the 'Save the Chicken Foundation' sponsors our fair. Imagine if I were putting the posters up myself. They'd be down so low that only the ants could read them," Hattie said, giggling.

"Perfect! Now everyone will see this," said Hattie. "We were fantastic together. Elliott, you applied the painter's tape perfectly so the sign is secure. Bentley, you helped me reach the flier so I was able to sign my name neatly. Thank you for helping. I don't think we'd have succeeded without you."

"You're welcome, Hattie. I'm happy that you didn't get too excited while you were signing the fliers. You might have jumped around and fallen off my head," Bentley answered.

I'm beginning to like helping people. It makes me feel much better inside than when I was a practicing bully. I never imagined I'd love doing things like escorting Hattie.

The Fair

Bentley thought, *I've been working on my secret project for weeks. I can't wait to unveil it at the fair today. In the meantime, I'll help set up Wooliam and Friends Lemonade Shack.*

"Wooliam, you look dashing in your new coat. I saw the colorful quilt that the Ladies Group of Sheep made from your wool. It's beautiful! Everyone will be impressed with it," said Bentley.

"Why thank you, Bentley," said Wooliam. He set up the cups and pitchers full of lemonade. "I'm wearing one of my fancy suit jackets today in honor of our fair."

"Hattie's running toward us with her bright yellow bonnet blowing in the wind. I wonder what she's excited about," said Bentley.

"Bentley, we have an emergency. Cherish Chicken is upset. She's afraid she can't sing in the talent show," said Hattie, hopping about. "Elliott is trying to calm her fears. It would be a pity if we couldn't help Cherish feel better so she could sing."

"Can we both hurry over to talk with her?" asked Hattie.

"Of course, Hattie, I'll come with you right away," Bentley answered. Bentley and Hattie rushed to the area where the talent show was being held.

***

"Cherish, what's wrong? Hattie told me you were afraid to sing in the talent show," said Bentley.

"Yes, I think everyone will laugh at me. Maybe they've never seen chicken wearing glasses. Besides, I might not be able to hit the high notes, even though I've been practicing faithfully every day," she said, trying to swallow her tears.

"Cherish, believe in yourself. It isn't as if you don't have the talent to sing. You're well prepared. You've been singing in the choir for some time and you're fabulous. You can do it. I know Elliott has already given you valuable advice, but I'd like you to remember my thoughts as well," said Bentley.

"Thanks for the compliment, Bentley. I've been trying to calm Cherish and build her confidence," said Elliott.

"I have an idea, Cherish. Instead of worrying about all the animals watching, just look at Elliott or me. Pretend no one else is in the audience. You know Elliott and I believe in you and we would never laugh at you," said Bentley. "By the way, I think your glasses look lovely."

"You've helped me more than I can say. I'm looking forward to doing my best in the talent show," said Cherish, managing a small smile. We'll be in the front row, cheering you on," said Elliott.

"I'm going to set up my surprise item for the fair. I'll see you later, Elliott," said Bentley as he trotted away.

On the day of the fair, Bentley walked around hunting for Hattie's booth.

"Hattie, your items look beautiful. Would you mind coming with me to see what I made for the fair? I'd like you to be the first to see it."

"I can't wait, Bentley," said Hattie, hopping about flapping her wings wildly. They hurried toward the "Save the Chicken Foundation" building.

"Bentley, it's magnificent. I never expected you to make a statue of me wearing a bonnet. What an honor," said Hattie, trying to regain her composure. "Thank you so much. How can I ever repay you?"

"Don't worry, Hattie, I wanted to do something nice to make up for the way I treated you when we first met," said Bentley. "After all, you're my first friend."

"I've forgiven you, Bentley. I know you weren't taught how to be thoughtful and kind. You have a good heart. You just didn't realize it then. You've become a wonderful friend," she added, patting him with her wing.

"I'm thrilled that you like it, Hattie. Now we must hurry back to the talent show so we don't miss Cherish singing her song," said Bentley. Hattie and Bentley arrived just before Sherman Sheep announced that she'd be the next one to perform.

"Presenting our next contestant, Cherish Chicken, singing about some of her favorite things," said Sherman Sheep.

Cherish Singing

Cherish walked on to the stage. She cleared her throat and glanced at the audience.

I'm looking straight at Bentley and Elliott. I can feel my legs shaking a little, but I'll do my best. I've worked hard for this moment. I finished my song. I must have done well. Everyone is standing and clapping. Bentley and Elliott are barking their approval. I can see Patsy Pig in the audience. Her face is covered with blueberries. I hope she didn't eat all of the pies.

"Attention, everyone, the judges have a hard decision to make," announced Sherman Sheep. "The contestants in the talent show were amazing. Congratulations to all of you. Here are the judges' choices: Third place goes to Carson Chicken for reciting the wonderful poem he created. Our second place award goes to Betty Lee Chicken for her marvelous tap dancing routine. Finally, our first place winner is Cherish Chicken for her beautiful song."

"Congratulations, Betty Lee and Carson, you are gifted," said Cherish.

"Thank you, Cherish, but you were the most amazing of all. We never knew you were a talented singer. We're going to ask you to sing at all of our events from now on," said Betty Lee.

"I'd be pleased to help whenever I can," said Cherish. "Let's celebrate by visiting Wooliam at his lemonade stand."

"That's a great idea. Wooliam and his friends make the most delicious lemonade," said Carson.

"Good afternoon, what can I do for you?" Wooliam asked, taking a bow.

"Wooliam, we would love some of your pink lemonade," said Betty Lee and Cherish together. "Your lemonade is delicious," said Cherish, carefully sipping her drink.

"I'd like some original flavor lemonade, please," said Carson.

"Certainly, Carson, here is your lemonade. I hope you enjoy it."

"It's delicious, Wooliam," said Carson, smacking his lips after sipping the sweet drink. "May I have some to take home to my family? I know they would love it. I can carry one of the plastic bottles around my neck," he added.

"Of course, Carson, please give my regards to your family," said Wooliam.

"I must stop by Hattie's booth. I 'd like to buy one of her adorable bonnets and purses," said Cherish.

"Good afternoon, Hattie," said Cherish. "You've nearly sold all your bonnets and purses. It's a good thing I came before you sold out. I'd love the pink set with ruffles. May I try it on?"

"Certainly, Cherish, please do," answered Hattie. "It looks darling on you. The pink color is beautiful next to your white feathers. Look into the mirror."

"Yes, it does look cute," said Cherish. "How much does it cost?"

"It's $2.50," Hattie replied. "I try to make all of my bonnets and purses reasonable so everyone can afford them."

"That's a fair price for such high-quality work," said Cherish. "In fact, I'd like to buy the blue plaid set for my mom. It will look beautiful on her and tomorrow happens to be her birthday," Cherish added. "She'll be thrilled."

"Thank you, Hattie. I'm excited about my new items. They're absolutely beautiful," said Cherish.

"I'll be happy to gift wrap them for you. I think your mom will be pleased," Hattie said.

"Here comes Bentley, waving a piece of paper. He's hurrying toward us," said Hattie.

"Hi Hattie, I wanted you to be the first to know the news. I'm still adding up our profits, but everyone exceeded their goals! Wooliam's quilt sold for $60. You've sold all your items, and Charlene has been busy signing her endearing books. A group of animals from the 'Save the Chicken Foundation' bought the statue. They want to put it outside their office to show everyone how grateful they are to you for arranging the fair", said Bentley. "Did you hear Sherman announce that I'm a reformed bully? He said now I'm a great example for the bully breeds. These include all kinds of bulldogs."

"Hattie, you'll wear yourself out from jumping around and your wings will be sore tomorrow from all of the flapping," Bentley warned.

"I'm beyond excited. The news is extraordinary," said Hattie, readjusting her bonnet. "I did hear part of the announcement from Sherman. I'm grateful that our team helped make our event such a success," Hattie added. "I owe a lot to all of you for being the best team ever."

Who will win the Kentucky Hunt Club Championship?

"Bentley, there are only two days before the Kentucky Hunt Club Show. Famous horses are coming from all around the country so Mary and I need to be at our best. I'm a bit nervous about it," said Charlene.

"Don't worry, Charlene, you and Mary have been working hard. Your efforts will pay off. I have every confidence in you," said Bentley.

"Thanks, Bentley, I feel better already. "

"You're most welcome, Charlene. I'm glad I'm not a bully anymore. I never did anything helpful then and I didn't know what it was like to have a friend. I missed a lot. But I'm concentrating on doing everything I can to be kind now, because I can't change all the dopey things I've done before," said Bentley. "If I hadn't become part of your winning team, I might've gotten the 'World's Biggest

Bully Award,' but that wouldn't have been something to celebrate."

***

Eva came into the barn carrying shiny blue-ribbon strips. "Charlene, I came by today to give you a wonderful bubble bath so you will look gorgeous for the show tomorrow. Then I'll braid your mane with these blue ribbons to give you a special touch. This show is especially important because when it's over the points will be added up and the winner of the High Score Award will be chosen. I think Mary will get a notification in the mail."

I'm happy Eva is here to help me look my prettiest. I think Judge and I might be battling for the trophy.

***

Charlene thought, *Elliott, Bentley and I are in the trailer on our way to the show. We're almost there now.* I *see big, colorful tents ahead. Some of them are for the horses that travel long distances; some are food tents. I wish the show was already finished. The suspense is making me nervous. But some people say that if you're a little nervous, it helps you do your best. I guess as long as my legs aren't shaking, I'll manage to do okay. I always look for positive things so today I'm grateful for the sunny weather. No splashing through the puddles.*

Mary is warming me up by taking some small jumps. I don't think I've ever seen so many horses in one place. It's a good thing they only allow one horse in the practice ring at a time; otherwise, they'd need a traffic cop.

"Ladies and Gentlemen, please come to ring one for the first Open Jumper Class," said the announcer. "Our first contestant will be number 203, Charlene the Star, ridden by Mary Harris."

This is it. Will I be able to jump my best? Judge isn't standing by the rail. I get especially nervous if he's watching. We're heading toward the oxer. Whew! We made it! Now there are three jumps close together. I need to jump them perfectly. No problem with that. We're heading for the stone wall. Yikes, my front foot touched it, but it didn't fall. The top of the stone wall can fall easily if you hit it, so I tried to be careful. We have only one post and rail jump left. We made it with no faults. I'm hopping up and down just a little to show everyone I'm happy. Elliott and Bentley are barking to show their approval.

"You were fantastic, Charlene. I'm proud of you. We can relax and watch the other horses now," said Mary, as she kissed Charlene's neck. "I put a peppermint in my pocket for good luck."

What a yummy reward. It pays to do my best. I might have to learn to do sit ups if I start getting too chubby, though.

"Ladies and gentlemen, Charlene the Star and Mary Harris had no faults. Congratulations to them," said the announcer. "Our next contestant I will be number eighteen, Presiding Judge, ridden by Kayla Moran.

Charlene thought, *I had a drink of water and some hay. I'm refreshed in case we have a jump-off. If we have a jump- off the course will probably be shorter with higher jumps. I'll have to pay attention.*

They just announced Judge had a clear round too, so we'll have a jump-off and Judge will be first. I'm watching him, pretending I'm not nervous. He never looks nervous. I wish I knew his secret. He isn't going fast. My job will be to try to go faster, without being careless.

Here we go. We're moving right along, but not crazy fast. Mary's telling me I should stretch out my stride so we can leave a stride out here and there. That way, we'll have a fast time. Mary is cutting the corners as short as she can, so we'll finish quicker. I must pay attention so the jumps don't take me by surprise. We're coming to the in and out. Ah, perfect. Next, we have the stonewall and the water jump. I tripped on the way to the water jump, but I recovered and didn't step into the water, or hit anything. I must keep up my speed to the last jump; the big oxer. I left out a stride. Oops, the rail is rattling around in the brackets, because I touched it with my hind foot. But it didn't fall.

"Ladies and gentlemen, our winner is number 203, Charlene the Star, ridden by Mary Harris. The time it took them to complete the course was thirty-five seconds, just two seconds faster than Presiding Judge. That was close to being another tie. Both horses and riders deserve a great deal of credit," said the announcer.

I heard the announcer say everyone who is entering the Open Jumper Under Saddle Class should go to ring two. When you enter an "Under Saddle" Class it means you don't jump. You just try to walk, trot and canter perfectly. A canter is a slow gallop. At the end of the class we all gallop faster and listen for the judge to say we should stop. We need to stop immediately because the judge will give us a higher score if we do things right away. Mary doesn't always enter this type of class, but she wants us to earn as many points as we can toward the High Score Award.

I feel the judge's eyes on me. I wonder if he'd be impressed if I smiled at him when we go by. The judge said, "All gallop, please" so we have go faster, without going crazy. *My friend Judge is here too. He seems* relaxed, but *not interested in stuff that doesn't involve jumping. When he cantered by me, he was yawning, so I guess he's bored. When he galloped by, I tried to flirt with him, but I don't think he noticed. I did make a little mistake. I should have been cantering, but I was trotting instead. I was right in front of the judge. Well, nobody's perfect.*

"Ladies and gentlemen, the judge has made is decision. First place, number 156, Jumpin' Jack ridden by Caroline Stone," said the announcer.

Too bad I made the mistake, but it's something I can work on next time. I don't remember who won second place, but I paid attention when they announced Judge won third place while Mary and I won fourth place. Mary's patting my neck, so I guess she's not too disappointed. She knows we're still a good team. I peeked over at the bleachers where Elliott and Bentley are sporting big smiles.

"Attention everyone, today our champion is number 203, Charlene the Star, ridden by Mary Harris with a total of seven points. Our reserve champion is number eighteen, Presiding Judge, ridden by Kayla Moran, with five points. It's been an exciting day for all of us," said the announcer. "We congratulate both horses and riders for their efforts."

"Charlene, look at this lovely trophy! You did a fine job today.

I think you've earned peppermints on top of your oats tonight," Mary said. "I can't wait to see who wins the High Score Award. You've learned a lot this year."

The Winner Is...

"Charlene, when will we know who won the High Score Award?" asked Hattie, flapping her wings. "I'm wearing my new blue bonnet for luck, in case we find out today. Hattie twirled so everyone could admire her new bonnet. "All of us are waiting for the news. Elliott is sitting outside crossing his paws. I wonder how he seems so calm. I'd hold my breath waiting for the news, but then I'd turn blue."

"Your new bonnet is exquisite, Hattie," said Charlene.

"Bentley, can I stand on your back? It'll give me a better view so I can see if Mary is coming with news for us," said Hattie.

"No problem, Hattie, I'd love to help you be the official look out while we're waiting for the news. But I hope you don't hop on me too much when you get excited," Bentley answered.

"Here she comes, everyone. She's running and waving a letter. I'll bet she has the results. I'd cross my fingers and toes if I could," said Hattie, flapping her wings wildly.

Charlene and her friends celebrating

"Charlene, you won." Mary shouted. "I can hardly believe you're the High Score Award winner. Your handsome friend, Presiding Judge, won Reserve Jumper High Score Award. I was so excited I forgot to mention that you won the class in the Kentucky Bluegrass Show the day we left early because you weren't feeling well. If we hadn't won that, Judge might have ended up with more points. Guess what else? Kayla was so impressed with your jumping skills that she's bringing Judge here for training. Isn't that great? You'll be able to see him more often."

Wow, it's hard to know what to be more excited about winning the High Score Award or getting to see Judge every day! Hattie is still hopping in circles. She's so thrilled. I hope she doesn't get dizzy. Bentley will have to run to her rescue again. Elliott is smiling and Bentley looks very pleased. Mary's going home to relax now.

"Congratulations, Charlene, I was listening from outside," Elliott said. "You're not only a champion because you won many awards this year, but you're always thinking of others and helping to make things better for them. You helped with the fair, even though you were not feeling well."

Bentley added, "Elliott has been an excellent coach for me. He never made me feel like a brat, even when I acted like one. He helped show me that I'd be a happier dog if I was thoughtful and kind. Now I've learned to be caring. I've also become more skilled at using my talents to help other animals. I might've neglected my math and masonry abilities forever if all of you hadn't reminded me I had them."

"I used to think I was only good at wearing bonnets. But now I know I have other talents. I can make hats and purses our friends love. We met Bentley and we taught him the value of friendship. All of us made a huge difference. Now we have a town full of cheerful chickens because of our fair," said Hattie. "I wonder what kind of adventure we can plan next. We'll have to start discussing the possibilities.

My goodness, I have a great idea. We can have a pie-eating contest at our next event. Imagine how happy Patsy Pig will be. She'll start eating pies right away to make sure she's the best when the have the event."

Take the Quiz

1. What was Bentley like when he first came?

2. What happened to Hattie when she found out her friends were sad? Why were they sad?

3. Who rescued Hattie when she heard her friends were depressed and what did he do?

4. What was Charlene's goal for this year? Did she reach her goal?

5. What happened to Charlene when she saw Presiding Judge while she was jumping in her class?

6. What did Bentley make for the fair?

7. Who won the talent show and who helped build her confidence when she was afraid?

8. What do you think is the main idea in this story?

Congratulations, you did a great job!

Answers:

1. Bentley was a bully when he came. He was rude and selfish.

2. Hattie nearly fainted when she found out her friends were sad. They were sad because they weren't having fun and they didn't feel talented.

3. Bentley ran to Hattie's side, to escort her to the chair.

4. She wanted to become the High Score Award winner. Yes, she reached her goal.

5. Charlene crashed through the jump when she first saw Presiding Judge.

6. Bentley made a statue of Hattie for the fair.

7. Cherish chicken won the talent show. Bentley and Elliott helped her feel less nervous so she could sing.

8. I think the main idea in the story is you can accomplish amazing things by working together and you can completely change your actions and thoughts, like Bentley did when he realized being a bully was wrong.

About the Author:

Deanie Humphrys-Dunne is an award-winning children's book author with six books published at this time: My Life at Sweetbrier, Charlie the Horse, Charlene the Star, Charlene the Star and Hattie's Heroes, Charlene the Star and Bentley Bulldog and Tails of Sweetbrier. All of her books offer positive messages for children, such as; setting goals, perseverance, sharing and friendship. Her sister, Holly Humphrys-Bajaj, beautifully illustrates all of Deanie's fictional books and designs the covers. The fictional stories are told by the memorable animal characters, who keep readers entertained with their endearing personalities. The animals find creative ways to help their friends. All books are available on Amazon and Barnes and Noble. You may also order signed copies from Deanie.

Her non-fiction story, *My Life at Sweetbrier,* is an inspirational award-winning memoir about a little girl whose one desire was to become a champion equestrian, in spite of her handicap. This book is a revised, expanded version of her first book, *Tails of Sweetbrier.*

Deanie is a graduate of the Institute of Children's Literature. Her books have won a number of awards and recognition including her latest awards for My Life at Sweetbrier; The gold medal in the New Apple Book Awards, and the gold medal in the Mom's Choice award, the Reader's Favorite silver medal, and two cover awards. Other awards are listed on Deanie's website.

More books by Deanie Humphrys-Dunne:

Charlie the Horse
Charlene the Star
Charlene the Star and Hattie's Heroes
and
My Life at Sweetbrier

Available on
http://childrensbookswithlifelessons.com/books-2/
and on Amazon.com

Check out our Website:
www.childrensbookswithlifelessons.com

Email: deanie@dhdunne.tk

90373225R00049

Made in the USA
Middletown, DE
23 September 2018